The Adventures of Sunny & The Chocolate Dog

Sunny & The Chocolate Dog Go to the Beach

Written by Susie Neimark
Illustrated by Kent Hammerstrom

Printed in Canada

ISBN# 0-9725945-1-5
LCCN# 2002095833

Written by Susie Neimark
Cover design & illustration by Kent Hammerstrom

Sunny & The Chocolate Dog, LLC
5 Palm Row, Suite C
St. Augustine, FL 32084

This book is dedicated to Jack.

May the happiness and love Sunny & Cloudy have shown us be shared and enjoyed by many others.

Special thanks to Kathy Tanaka, Tanya Husain, Kathleen Rowan, Courtney Goes, and, of course, Sunny & Cloudy (The Chocolate Dog) for the inspiration they have provided.

Today was a very special day for Sunny and Cloudy. Sunny had been dreaming about this day for weeks and weeks, and now it was here. They were going to go to the beach! Sunny was especially excited because today she was going to help teach her new little sister, Cloudy, how to swim and play in the sand.

Sunny had gone to the beach many times with her mommy and daddy, but she had never been there with Cloudy. You see, Cloudy was just a baby last summer - much too young for an adventure to the beach. And when she became old enough to go, the summer had already ended, so they all had to wait patiently for the chilly winter days to pass. Now, the warm, sunny days had finally arrived, and it was time for the whole family to go to the beach!

Sunny and Cloudy were very excited about their trip to the beach. But before they could be on their way, there were lots of supplies their mommy and daddy needed to pack into their beach bag to bring along. They packed things like beach toys to play with, fresh water for drinking, sunscreen to prevent sunburns, and a first-aid kit just in case anyone got an ouchie. Once they had gathered all the necessary supplies to have a safe and fun day at the beach, it was time to go at last!

Uh oh, one more thing! Before they could leave for the beach, Mommy and Daddy had to go over some very important rules with Sunny and Cloudy. "While at the beach, you both must always be with an adult or a partner, and NEVER by yourself - especially in the water," said their daddy. "It's called the buddy system."

Mommy explained, "Sometimes there can be waves that might push you all around, and sometimes it can suddenly get deep." "Even good swimmers need to be extra careful," said their daddy. "It is always safer when you are with a buddy and not alone - just in case one of you gets hurt or lost." Finally, after all of the rules had been explained, it was really time to go to the beach!

On their way to the beach, they took a nice walk through some beautiful parks and playgrounds where the sisters got to stop and watch the squirrels and see all of the children playing. Sunny and Cloudy were very excited to get to the beach, but they couldn't help taking just a few minutes to have some fun in the park.

The kids on the playground were so happy to see Sunny and Cloudy coming that they ran right over to them and gave them lots of hugs and kisses. The children knew that today was Cloudy's first time going to the beach and that she was going to learn how to swim. "Good Luck, Cloudy!" they shouted as they waved goodbye.

Sunny and Cloudy knew that they were getting closer to the beach because they could hear the waves and smell the water. Their tails wagged and wagged with anticipation. Finally, their exciting journey through the park was over, and they arrived at the entrance to the beach. "We're here, we're here!" said Sunny excitedly.

Sunny and Cloudy could hardly wait to get on the beach where they saw all of the other dogs playing in the sand and swimming in the water. "Come on guys, faster!" said Sunny. The two of them pulled on their leashes to try to get their mommy and daddy to hurry, but their mommy reminded them that they needed to stay close by, especially since it was Cloudy's first visit to the beach.

Once they got on the sand, the girls ran straight to the edge of the water so that Sunny could start teaching Cloudy how to swim right away. Sunny told Cloudy that there was nothing to be scared of and to just take it slowly – just like Sunny did when she first learned how to swim. "You are going to love swimming, Cloudy!" said Sunny.

Sunny stayed right next to Cloudy - just in case her little sister got nervous. Their mommy and daddy stood close by too, watching both of them. As soon as the girls reached the shore, a couple of dogs ran over to give Cloudy their support and encouragement. "Hi guys! This is Cloudy, my little sister. I am teaching her how to swim today," said Sunny.

At last, Cloudy worked up enough courage to take her first step - just barely touching the water. Suddenly, along came a small wave and splashed her right in the face. "Oh, dear! Nobody told me that was going to happen!" shouted Cloudy.

Cloudy quickly turned around and ran away from the water, straight to her mommy and daddy. They comforted her and told her that it was okay to be scared. Her daddy said that she could try again later when she was ready. "Don't let that little old wave frighten you, Cloudy. We won't let you get hurt," said Sunny.

Sunny noticed that some dogs were catching balls and sticks in the water. Sunny asked her daddy if she could get a toy out of their beach bag so that she and Cloudy could play like the other dogs. Cloudy decided to let Sunny do this by herself, and sat close by her mommy to see what Sunny was going to do with the toy.

Sunny picked up one of the toys in her mouth and dropped it by her daddy's feet for him to throw for her. He threw it way out into the water, and Sunny took a running start, jumped into the water, and swam as fast as she could towards her toy. She paddled and paddled with her paws until she finally reached her toy. She grabbed the toy in her mouth and brought it back to her daddy to throw again.

Cloudy sat on the beach and carefully watched Sunny play in the water. She wished that one day she would be able to swim just like Sunny. She watched as her daddy threw the toy into the water again for Sunny. This time he threw it even farther, but it was still no problem for Sunny. She was a great swimmer.

Sunny swam far out into the water to retrieve the toy and brought it back to her daddy to throw again. But this time he asked Cloudy if she would like to try and get the toy. Cloudy wanted so very much to be able to swim and get toys from the water like Sunny, but she was still scared.

Sunny told Cloudy that she had to try and practice, or else she would never learn how to swim. Then Sunny had an idea! She picked up her toy, walked over to the edge of the water, and dropped it in the shallowest part. "Okay Cloudy, let's start here," said Sunny.

Cloudy looked at the toy. It was floating in the water just a few inches away from her reach. She was sure she could get it! Slowly, she took a couple of steps into the water. At first, she was a little startled because the water was a bit cold, but that wasn't going to stop her. Then she carefully bent down and grabbed her toy. Everyone was so proud of her, especially Sunny. "Way to go, Cloudy!" cheered Sunny.

Cloudy had done such a good job that this time Sunny picked up the toy, swam a little further out into the water, and dropped it again. Cloudy was not quite sure if she could go out that far yet. She looked back at her mommy, then she looked at her daddy, and then she noticed that all the other dogs were watching and cheering for her. "You can do it, Cloudy! Go Cloudy!" shouted all of the other dogs.

Suddenly, after just a few steps into the water, Cloudy found herself paddling and paddling without even realizing she was swimming. She looked back and saw that everyone was clapping and cheering for her. She was doing it! She was swimming!

Cloudy was so excited that she swam right passed her toy and continued to swim until she heard the others calling her back. "Cloudy, come back! You passed your toy!" shouted Sunny. Cloudy turned around and headed back to the shore, grabbing her toy on the way.

When she finally reached the shore, her family and all the other dogs greeted her with excitement and praise for all that she had accomplished. They were all so very proud of her, and Cloudy was also very proud of herself. She got a big hug from her mommy and daddy.

From that moment on, nothing could keep Sunny or Cloudy out of the water when they were at the beach, especially Cloudy. They would play in the water with their beach toys, and sometimes they would even help other dogs learn how to swim. So, now every warm summer morning, the girls ask their mommy and daddy, "Can we go to the beach today, please?"

Join the Sunny & The Chocolate Dog Pen Pal Club!!!

How many dogs do you know who have their very own email address?
Well, Sunny and Cloudy do!
One of their favorite things to do is to write to their friends, so email them a
message or a question, and they will write back!
If you are a pen pal, Sunny and Cloudy will also tell you when they have gone on
a new adventure so that you can read all about it.

Sunny and Cloudy even have their own website with fun facts, puzzles and games
too!

Visit Sunny and The Chocolate Dog at: www.sunnyandthechocolatedog.com

Go on another adventure with Sunny & The Chocolate Dog

Sunny Meets Her Baby Sister
ISBN# 0-9725945-0-7

Sunny & The Chocolate Dog Go To The Doctor
ISBN# 0-9725945-2-3